I0572430

I LOVE MY PLATE FULL

I LOVE MY PLATE FULL

BY

KENO KICEASE

Published by
Wikked Konnection Publishing
A subsidiary of Vantage Point Media, LLC
3416 N. Shadeland Ave.
Indianapolis, IN 46226

Second Printing

PUBLISHER'S NOTE

ISBN 978-0-9837771-3-7

Printed in the United States of America

Keno, is a writer of Erotic Poetry and Short stories inspired by his love for full figured women.

I Love My Plate Full
Not only do his words stimulate the mind but intensify the soul.

His inspiration does not stop at just full figure women but his love for all women...

Acknowledgements

This book is dedicated to my father, Arthur Waldo who started me reading at the age of three; therefore developing my love for reading and writing.

Verda Waldo, my mother for teaching me how to love women for who they are.

Laura Queen Collier

Toya Torres

Dawn Dandridge

To all my sisters: Sherrie, Ivy, Boka, Simone

To every full figured woman that I have had the pleasure of knowing.

Keno's Glossary

Panties- Something that I pull to the side so I can get to the sweet good pussy

Thongs- Something that is even easier for me to pull to the side and hit the pussy from the back

Bra- Something I pull off women so I can put those heavy breasts in my mouth

Half A Gallon or Gallon of Milk- Breasts

Aphrodisiac- A big sexy woman in a sexy negligee

Yummy- Wide hips and big ass on a full figured woman

Working- When a big gal is walking down the streets and her backside is jiggling

Beautifully Crafted- The way JAH made the full figured woman

An A.P.E- Accomplished pussy eater

Pussy- Passion Fruit, Ripe Fruit, Pussy, Pussy, Sugar walls, Rivers of the Nile

Juices- The womanly waters that run down thighs and legs when a woman comes has an orgasm

Tashi- Dick, Man wood, Pipe

Bumpy Circles- Areolas

Housebroken or Housebound- Pussy whipped

Hit and Run- A fuck

Rodeo- When a woman is on top riding you

Manage- Being able to handle a full figured woman in the bed

Nightcap- Sex before bedtime

No-Show- When your penis won't get hard.

Moisture- Something that happens between a woman's thighs after reading my erotic writings

Strongback- Something needed when you deal sexually with a full figured woman

Woodwork- A blowjob

Dick on cut- With a rubber

Dick Raw- Without a condom

Facial- When a man's face is wet with juices from eating a woman

False Ideas- What somebody tells you something you want to hear so they can get something from you.

Visit Again- To go back and have sexual relations with someone again

The Fire has burnt out- When you no longer love somebody or loses feelings for someone.

Appetite- When you have an immense desire to be oral with someone

Advertisement- When a woman shows a lot of breast or ass as in clothing

Special Occasions- Two days really, the day you meet someone and the first day y'all made love

I LOVE MY PLATE FULL

Guilty as Charged

I am guilty as charged of loving the fuller woman, the bigger woman, the one type of woman who when she walks by, makes men shake their head and say, 'DAMN!'

I am guilty of keeping thoughts of her in my head, that bigger woman, that more lovable woman with so much more to love.

I am guilty of loving the more sizable woman, the woman that is a product of gravy, fried chicken, and corn bread. That afternoon snack and delicious dessert type woman.

I am guilty of loving the thicker woman, the "its" so satisfying snickers type of woman. "That what would you do for a Klondike", "Taste the rainbow" between her legs.

Starburst type woman.

I am guilty of loving that plump woman, hips that make you want to do the bump type woman. Her ass so big, it was imported from BA-DUNK Island type woman.

 Impressively large breast, "Hershey Kiss" size nipple type woman.

When I come up for air, my face and beard shining with her juice type woman.

I am guilty, guilty

I am guilty, guilty

and guilty as charged…Your Honor.

Advice from your man's best friend

Let me tell you something about your man, my best friend. He's my best friend, but he doesn't deserve you. He is running around chasing this skinny twig type women, when he has a full-figured goddess like you at home. A woman I would fill my day and complete my night with.

He's my best friend and he tells me how he doesn't hug or caress you. I would pay attention to those needs, I'd love to hug that big soft body and caress and rub your sexy curves, stretch marks included. Warm oil foot massages when you come in from work and kick off your shoes.

He's my best friend, and he says your butt is too big. To me it's a butt very great in size and as I sit on this couch looking at it, I would love to have my lap weighted down with all of that.

He's my dog, my man, my best friend, and he tells me that your breasts are too big and saggy. He doesn't like touching them, he prefers a perky pair of A or B cups.

Me, I would love to feel your large breasts in my hands. My motto is bigger is better…

If you have big nipples, that's just more for my tongue to play with. If you happen to have large areolas, well I think that is so sexy.

He's my right hand man, me brethren, my best friend and he says he hates any type of bed activity with you. He says you're just good for oral sex. I say sex with a big gal is a work out that he's not built for. He's not capable of handling the large work load.

From where I'm sitting, it look likes underneath all those clothes you have on, you have the works (*breast, hips, backside, and legs*), and he can't handle it. I tell him to leave off the bed! He says when you position for doggie style, your butt spreads out and it's too wide for him. I tell him, you can't handle it, leave off the bed!

I can stay on the bed because I can handle the large and big things JAH has blessed you with.

He's my comrade, my roadie, my best friend and he says he is going to leave you soon. I say when he does, you call me up. I would love to fill that vacancy in your life and bedroom. I can give your body that night time care that it needs. I can satisfy you in every aspect of your life and he can be your new man's best friend.

On You and for You

I had been seeing her for months, so I said to her in a ganja induced vocal.

Let me use some sexy words on you. Like every time I see you. I'm like JAH! Arranged in you, in the form of a full figured goddess, anything you wear sweetheart, you wear it well.

These streets are just a big stage for you to showcase your big legs, thighs, breast, and forgive me for being blunt, but your ass too! I like the way your chest bubbles out of the top of your bra, it looks sexy. A nice chunky piece of work, your front structure is nice to look at, and you have a nice big backyard. You definitely manifest the image of a big sexy woman and there is no way to avoid looking at you when you walk by.

You make 'bigger is better' a fact, not fiction. Look at the way men are leaning out of their car windows, to get a better glimpse of you. Like me, they are starving for a meal like you.

And now I see your bus is coming. Look, maybe you can come over and let me make you a dish of jerk chicken, rice and peas, yams and cabbage, and wash it down with a bottle of peanut punch, would you like that? We will make it happen one day.

Alright, may the rest of your day be blessed. See you.

All in the Family

One day my brain said to my mouth, "Yo, the ears gave me some bad news today." The mouth asked what it was. The brain said, "You know that girl that dick sexed last month, well turns out she is pregnant." Mouth said, "You sure the ears heard right?"

Brain thought about the stupid ass question mouth had just asked and said, "I was right there asshole!" Mouth said, "The asshole is in the back, remember."

And by the way, why didn't you tell me this earlier? Matter of fact, why you telling me about this anyway?" Brain said, "It wouldn't have happened, if you didn't try to talk to every big gal with big legs, big ass, and big breast that you see."

Mouth kissed teeth and said, "You need to talk to eyes about that one."

Eyes heard that and said, "Don't blame us, true we like to see jeans stuffed with what we call a whole heap of ass; yes we like to see breast so big, it's difficult for a bra to control them, but when we see a body like that, you brain, start lusting and get all in the ears. Next thing I know, mouth you talking and after that you are getting cell phone numbers and such."

Keno who had been drinking a lot of water that day, went to the bathroom to take a leak, as soon as he unzipped his pants, here come dick popping out, throwing up a whole bunch of water.

Dick shook himself dry and said, "I am in my apartment (*pants*) with my windows *(zipper)* shut, I can hear y'all garbling." Brain, ears, eyes, and mouth looked down and said all together, "You are the main reason we are in this trouble."

Dick said, "Oh no if it wasn't for y'all three, I wouldn't be able to do shit, no offense asshole in the back! I am the last player off the bench in this game. Matter of fact, blame the hands, they always supposed to put my jacket on before I go into wet places. Hand did not say a damn thing, but brain said, 'Oh I forgot, my bad!'"

Dick said, "Shoot, I would like to go in sometimes and take my time but the fingers get all in the pussy playing with her so by the time he pulls me out, and pushes me in, it is all wet and juicy and tight, until I cannot help but to bust!"

Brain sent signals to the mouth and they both said, "Damn, the pussy does be good don't it?"

They were all in agreement with that one; They were all in the family.

In One Ear and Out the Other

I keep telling these dudes how to keep their women happy, but they don't want to listen. I have studied women. I went to kindergarten, grade school, junior high, high school, and college concerning women. I sat up late at night and got up early in the morning concerning women. I learned the hot spot, right spot, g spot, and the get it real wet spot and dig it, some of the times, they are not the same spot.

Every time your woman kisses you, don't necessarily mean they want a dick between their thighs. Sometime they just want to be cuddled and held. Now you might laugh and say I am talking shit, but that's why men like me are loving women of yours.

Sometime they want the foot massage, neck massage, and a back rub.

Cut off the lights, light the candles, and have warm water in the tub. And when she comes out the tub, have a towel ready and waiting for her. Throw the towel down and use your tongue. You say a wet tongue can't dry a body...un un!

I have a special technique. You act like all you need is good dick, man please!

Its brothers out there that are attentive, caring, and faithful, plus good dick.

When they buck up on your gal, where are you going to be? Out in the damn cold!

You want to go up in her and 'beat it up' as you say. Brother man, I got five dick thrust styles:

1. Charge left and right

2. Pull up then plunge down.

3. Push in real slow and pull out the same way.

4. Thrust your dick deep and then pull out and tease her with your dick head.

5. Push the dick deep and grind the pelvis.

The technique depends on the type of woman with which you are dealing. I keep telling you, if you have the good dick, without being attentive and caring to her; It's like cookies and no milk, dry ass peanut butter and no jelly, it's just not working. So as long as it's in one ear and out the other, you will always lose your girl to the real thorough ass brothers.

100% African Wood(Tashi)

Listen up big gals and women!

I got the good stuff. The best drug out there, females are shot the hell out.

Show me a female, who once she got a hit of it wouldn't want more and I show you a liar. It's known by word of mouth, they say it's a terrible thing the way these women get hooked on it. I got it fat and brown and I keep it wrapped in its rubber package.

Wrapped up, so come and get some.

Listen up big gals and women!

I got the good stuff. If you could take one thing to bed with you tonight, and the next day, and the day after that, it would be this stuff.

Tashi, for life!

I cannot help but to push Tashi. Women on their beds closed eyes and opened mouths, loving every thrust and stroke of Tashi. Thrust deeply from side to side, what is it…

It's Tashi!

Making your bedsprings squeak. Making your bed sheets wet from it. Your juices running down your thighs and all over your back side, what's the cause of it…

It's Tashi!

It'll make thick and big women sing the big gals anthem, and it goes like this:

"Oh yes baby, right there, Oh yes, don't come yet I'm almost there!" What is it?

It's Tashi!

Coming to a town near you real soon.

When it gets there, leave work early or just call out. It's worth the wait.

What is it?

Tashi!

The what?

Tashi!

Big gals run for what?

Tashi!

A Wonderful Thing

Not only did I leave with your kiss on my lips, I also left with your name in my mouth because every time I opened my mouth up, your name jumped out.

People said I must really feel you because your name stayed on my lips and dominated my conversation. I'm always talking about you, thinking about you, it has become natural for me.

When I pull out from in between your thighs and out of your loving,

When I zip my pants up and leave out of your house and start walking,

I feel you on my manhood, still throbbing for your warm place. I say to myself, damn!

I could never cheat on you, my mind wouldn't allow it, my heart wouldn't hear of it and my dick would become soft and limp if I tried to put it in the next woman's pussy.

I have never had a woman have this type of effect on me. I hope I have finally found my queen, my eve and my soul-mate. My match -- mentally and sexually.

I guess I can say the words "I love you." This is what it must feel like; it feels good to think about a person a lot. When you see other women, you see that person. When you hear other women speak, you hear that person's voice. Love is a Wonderful Thing!

What does a Moka want?

Moka do you need my hands? Though small they are strong enough to catch you if are you falling. They are soft enough to massage your body when you are tired. They are caring enough to run your bath water when you want to soak and relax in the tub.

Moka do you need my eyes? They are there to look at your big and sexy curves. They are there to admire everything about you, from your wide hips, all the way up to your massive breast.

Moka do you need my ears? They are there to hear how rough your day at work was. When I am not attentive and caring enough they are ready hear that too.

Moka do you need my mouth? It is there to suck your Hershey Kiss size nipples. It is there to tell you how much I love and need you. It is there to whisper sweet things in your ears and bite lightly on your ear lobe.

Moka, do you need my stiff manhood? It is here to plunge slowly and deeply into your love split, place it between your thighs for me. It is here to move in and out of you causing you to orgasm, to let your juices to flow down your thighs and soak your bed, leaving evidence of our intense love-making.

Moka do you need me?

Because I need you!

Needing some Pleasure Part One

Cyn woke up to her alarm clock blasting KYW New 1060. She rolled over and three red numbers saying six o'clock was staring her in the face. She was off today, but had forgotten to cut the alarm off the night before. She got up and did the thing (brushed her teeth, pee, wash, etc.)

When she came out of the bathroom and walked back into her room, she caught a glimpse of herself in one of her many mirrors. She had mirrors on her ceiling and all around her room as well as the walls. She had paid a couple of dollars to have that shit done. Whenever and where ever she had a dick up in her she wanted to see it. In her room she could see herself get it in any and every position.

She had this whole thing done last year and in that time she had only taken advantage of it five times. She had kicked her boyfriend of three years out after she had got her mirrors set up. For three years his stroke game had never improved, matter of fact it never did anything, he could barely get hard and he came too fast, he just had a sad working dick.

Now even though she was twenty-eight and he was forty-five, she had loved him so she tried to overlook his problems. She went out and brought a dildo, a nice fat black one. When he couldn't, and he never did satisfy her, she would roll over and put black "Jimmy", as she called it, to work and he always handled his business.

She got tired of her man using his age as an excuse to hide that he was secretly smoking rocks and she finally put his ass out,

But anyway, she was looking at herself in the mirror, "Damn!" she thought. Her titties were big as shit, her long overnight shirt did little to hide them. She grabbed one of the heavy things and squeezed, "Oh Shit!" She whispered.

"This feels good, it needs a warm mouth." Cyn threw her night shirt off and took her two hands and brought one of her big breast to her mouth. She teased herself first by using her tongue and circling her areolas as her nipples got hard and erect. She then her put nipple and areola into her mouth and sucked. The fact she was watching herself in the mirror brought extra excitement. "Oh Damn, I need a dick so bad, I am going out of my fucking mind. All of this big and soft, all tight, about to be wet and nobody to hit it", she said to herself. She alternated sucking and licking both tits.

Between her legs were starting to get wet and an aroma that said it's jumping down here, the pussy that is, and it needed something in it: Something with length, something hard preferably with veins. Cyn brought her hand to her pussy and started rubbing her outer lips. She backed up to her bed and layed down. She pulled her hood back and exposed her fat clitoris. The pussy was calling for black Jimmy, if you cannot get the real dick, get the next best thing. Cyn rolled over and got black Jimmy from the drawer out the night table, next to the bed. That is what she loved about him, always hard and ready to work.

Needing some Pleasure Part Two

She went back to the position on her back and spread her legs open. With her right hand, the middle finger, she played with her clit and with her left hand; she rubbed the fat head of Jimmy, on the outer lips of her pussy. She noticed the head of Jimmy starting to become wet from her outer lips. As her breathing became shallow, she could not take it anymore and slowly pushed Jimmy's length into her pussy. She would push it in half way and pull out all the way, to the head, and push it back in again.

She repeated until before she knew it, she was fucking herself with all eight inches of black Jimmy. She moved her hips to meet the thrusts of her hand and Jimmy. It got to feeling so good, that she raised her hips off the bed to catch that force moving in and out of her pussy. Every time Jimmy came out, it was shining with her juices which included popping sounds of her pussy being fucked by Jimmy.

Cyn closed her eyes and imagined it was that sexy dread Fire she had met on the Ave. The one she gave her number to so he could call her. She thought next time I want his dick taking black Jimmy's place. "Oh My, Oh Damn, I am coming, oh yea, hit it black Jimmy, this is your pussy today!" Cyn was singing those words like it was a hit song. She felt pleasure rise from somewhere like an invisible ghost had grabbed and shook her…Her thighs and legs quivering. With her legs still spread open and each of her hands grabbing bed sheets, and black Jimmy between her thighs, Cyn shook enjoying her orgasms with her wetness, leaving evidence of her pleasure on the bed sheets. Damn, she thought next time I need a real dick.

Been a Member Since

This is a letter to all those fake ass dudes, who all of a sudden claim they got love for the full-figured woman. I hear their conversations on the buses and trains.

Talking about "Man big Joins be having that paper, they keep money in their account and they don't mind breaking you off." I hate those types of dudes and it is not even about the size of a woman. I hate for any woman to be taken advantage of and manipulated by evil hearted, weak ass, lying and cheating fake ass dudes.

They're trying to get their 'I love a big gal' membership on false pretenses.

Me, I have been a member since my teens, big gal addict, addicted only to the thick, big bone, heavy, voluptuous, 170 lbs and up. By late teens, I was proudly displaying my membership; I had gotten a taste of a big gal loving. My first juicy pussy, it was true what my uncles had said, "Jump in and get wet in between big gal thighs and you want to swim forever." From then until now my motto is bigger is better.

You can have the string bean thin gal, but me I need a heavy dose of big gal loving. These fake ass dudes trying to play my full-figured Queens, STOP IT! I have been a member since way back. Love the big breast and ass in abundance, sexy face, the softness of fullness of the body. When the creator was distributing backside and breast and hips, the women that kept getting back in line, YEA! That is how I like them.

Y'all fake ass dudes with fake love and bad intentions when it comes to the full-figured Goddess, I burn ya with gasoline and fire. I revoke y'all membership, Y'all get the steel toe boot, y'all playing, I been a member since the time I laid my head on some big soft thighs and had my face mashed up against large soft breast.

Like Biggie said, "I am not only a client but here I am also the president."

This is my duty to expose fake dudes to my full body Queens, cause like I said, I been loving y'all and I been member since way back when.

The Battle of the Sexes Part One

We started as soon as the sunlight crept through our half opened blinds and introduced us to the morning. It was cold and windy outside but our room was warm and cozy. My lady must have been playing with herself earlier because by the time she rolled over and straddled me her pussy was wet, tight, and warm. I had an early morning erection hard as an aluminum bat. I had my eyes closed, faking sleep, when I heard and felt her easing slowing down on my hardness. With both of her hands on my shoulders she pushed down and all of my fat eight went up in her. She put her mouth to my ear and flicked her tongue in there and then she bit lightly on my earlobe.

She whispered in my ear, "Baby why you faking, you woke up the same time your dick did, this early morning dick feels good all in me." I opened my eyes up and did not say anything. She knew I did not speak until I brushed my teeth. I did not talk with yuck mouth and bad breath. For some reason, hers never smelled. She looked at me and said, "you want to brush your teeth hun? Am I too heavy for you, you know this is a big gal you are working with. Lift me up and take me to the bathroom, so you can brush your teeth." She knew I would respond to the challenge. I lifted her up off the bed and she wrapped her big soft legs tight around my waist. I carried her like she was one of those big heavy boxes I'd unload off the trucks at my job. I slow walked us to the bathroom.

Her large breast was smashed all up against my face, blocking my view so I made it to the bathroom strictly on memory. Now through all of this, we were in a slow grinding fuck. Once in the bathroom, I set the part of our melted bodies which just happened to be her ass on the edge of the sink. Now even while I was grinding up in her pussy, she was still rolling her hips like she was twirling an invisible hula-hoop, my dick still pushed deep in her.

I rinsed my mouth and then I brought my lips to hers. I licked her top lip, then her bottom lip lightly like I was licking a Popsicle sideways. Her lips were slightly opened and I took my hard tongue and slowly pushed it in her mouth like my dick had pushed in her pussy minutes ago. I lifted her off the sink; our lips still locked and carried her back to the bed. I had to lay her on the bed and hit this big stuff right. I wanted to start my morning off proper, plus I needed to work off this built up sperm. We hadn't done anything in two days.

I laid her down on the bed, our bodies still melted together. I took my mouth off hers and went to her ear. I wanted to repay her for earlier. I flicked my tongue in and out her ear and sucked on her earlobe. As I made my way down to her neck, I heard her moaning. I stand sucking lightly at her neck before returning to her lips.

We deep tongued and kept our passionate kissing engaged. I pulled from off her lips and brought my lips to her breast. I was in my zone, wasn't too many brothers messing with me when it came to me sucking breast. I had that thing on lock, no fuck it, I had it on deadbolt. Now my lady was pushing some triple "D's" which is a "F" cup, trust me I know stuff like that, that is why I stay requested for but I am into my babe and don't want to and wouldn't cheat anyway, but back to the breast. I pulled each breast up and licked under them, most guys do not pay attention to that part of the breast. I then came full circle around until I was near the nipple. I licked around the areola of both breasts, which by now my baby had pushed together.

I took both nipples in my mouth at the same time and did that thing I do with my tongue. Now all the while I am on my titty project, I am still length deep in her pussy. I heard her breathing become shallow now and she was sweating. She took her hands off her breast and grabbed my ass cheeks and pulled me more into her as if that was even possible.

Her pelvis was moving into circular motion, as was my dick too. The way she rolled her pelvis, my dick was moving like the minute hand of a clock, only it was moving around in her pussy. It was wet and now it was starting to pop as some air must have snuck between our tools of loving-making below. I felt pressure build up in my man-hood so I grinded even harder, applying more pressure. I did not have any more dick left because it was all in her. It felt good, DAMN! I tried not to think about it but my mind noticed it too and said, "Damn black man this pussy is wet as all get out, it got me in a snug and warm fit. Fuck it! We are about to bust!" I added speed and intensity and that is when it hit my dick and shot out from us with such force.

It had the pressure of being backed up for two day. It hit into her pussy and that is what set her off. I felt her body spasm, her thighs were shaking and her nails dug deep into my back with force. As she was coming, I stopped my movement. My hard dick was inside of her still and I stopped moving, so she could enjoy that orgasm.

Take notes fellas. That's what you do when your girl starts cumming. After she came and stopped shaking, we stayed in the position of me on top and she on the bottom. I ran my fingers through her hair and kissed her. She was glowing and she looked beautiful in her natural state, her raw essences. I then realized like I always did I love this chick and I was not going anywhere.

You Lose Something?

I got a phone call last night and when I answered this is
what I heard at the other end of the line, "Yo, I just snuck and
looked at my woman's cell phone bill and this fucking number is
all over the page. I want to know who the fuck are you? This is my
woman, Dick!"

I put my first response which would have been anger in
check because in a calm voice, I was going to mentally fuck his
mind up. I said in a calm and controlled voice, "Look you low self-
esteem, not doing anything for her, fake example of a black man.
The woman you see may look like your woman, talk like your
woman, have wide hips, fat back side, and large juicy breast like
your woman but that is not your woman.

Your woman left seven months after meeting me. The
woman's who house you put your key into and turn the lock to
open is my woman. Think about it, in the last seven months, what
have you done for her sexually? It's only been oral right? I mean
you can eat all you want but your penis has been put on the status
of retirement. As far as her loving is concerned, your wood work
is unemployed with no chance of being rehired.

And as one black man to a next black boy, I call it like I see
it, the dick was not reason you lost her. It was the fact that since
she is a big woman, you felt like she had to accept anything.
Accept other women calling her house late at night. Accept your
lies, your deceit, your chronic cheating; she did not have to accept
it because a real man was waiting in the wings. Waiting to give her
all the attention plus some other stuff she needed. Waiting to love
her for her, her ways, her likes and dislikes her body and her kids.
These are the reasons you lost her and I found her. Finders keeper
losers' weepers! Even now she's sleeping right? Lean over and

whisper, Keno in her ear then sit up and watch her nipples get hard. Wait a next minute, then whisper the name in her ear, Tashi (*Swahili for me, but that is what I call my dick.*) and watch even in a deep sleep as her legs and thigh spread apart. Wait a next minute, you will smell something. That is the aroma from between her legs because her loving is awaiting Tashi's arrival. Now put a finger down there and it will be soaking wet, that is the type of effect I have on her mind, body, and not her soul, JAH has that. I have it on lock, and on lock down. Add county, state, and fed time, that is how much time she is going to do with me.

Now what you can do is hang up the phone, don't call me again and enjoy the limited time you have with my woman. Take this lesson over to your next relationship and remember to give her the love, attention, and respect you did not give your woman who became my woman, Good Night!"

Bedroom Secrets

If I were in your bedroom and asked it some questions, what would it reveal to me? What secrets is it keeping? Would it tell me there was another man here the other night, loving that big soft body of yours? The body I thought was mine, the body you said was for my eyes, hands, mouth, and dick only?

Would your bedroom reveal that it and the stuffed animals in the room were an audience to you and the other man's mashing of bodies. Would it say the other man's *bedrock* was better than mines, loving that big soft body of yours which I thought was mines. Would it play back the sounds of you and the other man? The sounds it had recorded. The sounds of the other men all up in your sweet pussy which I thought was my pussy, beating it up in my, in our bedroom. What secrets would it reveal and your walls…what would they say? Would they say, "Damn homey, the next man was beating that thing up, he had her hopping and hollering, bawling out. He was giving her slow long strokes and she was pledging herself to him and his dagger".

I sit in your bedroom, it smells different. It feels different. I look at your bed; sheets are thrown around all crazy on the bed. I wonder what secrets your bed is keeping from me. Would it reveal how the other man was slamming all up in your loving, I thought was mine? Would it tell me all the positions he had you in: Doggy style, back shot, wheel barrel, sideways slant and you on top? Damn! You are a star when you are on top riding, that's your shot. It pains me to know that another man had you screaming to our walls, on our bed, in our bedroom. What secrets would they reveal…The walls, the bed, and the bedroom, if they could only speak…

Tashi on the Loose

Tashi said to me, "Unzip this zipper and set me free. The only time you let me out is for the hand to touch me and it might feel good but it doesn't feel right. I need something wet and warm, preferably with a split, oh yes it has to be tight. I want you to get a big body woman. They have the good stuff, the best stuff, the type of stuff that as soon as I get in, I start throwing up but it's cool, don't worry just pull me out smack and shake me and I'm hard and ready to go again.

"Tashi said to me, "Unzip this zipper and let me loose from this cage. I'm like a wild animal and I need fresh meat, thick meat, big and soft, a chunky piece of work, that thick meat. Nix the hand, I'm beat free tonight. I don't care how big the breasts are, the mouth and tongue can handle that. I don't care how wide the hips are, that's the hands department. But me, I want the thighs thick or fat, I want the pussy fat.

Don't bring me anything under 160lbs, make me punch you in the stomach if you do that. "Tashi said to me, "Unzip this zipper and set me free. I want to push push in the cush." It could be bald, lightly shaved or a hairy bush. Make sure the backside is fat and can jiggle like Jell-O when I hit it. You know I sometimes like to come to the front from the back and if she is throwing it back to me hard, I'm throwing it right back; I will not retreat. I want to explore my options, all the positions, all of them entertaining.

When I'm done we can sit back and look at her on the bed knocked out.

" So unzip this zipper and Set Tashi Free."

Champion

There was a five foot nine, two hundred and ten pound stacked twenty-eight year old female who lived on our block. Her name was Klareese. She had butter pecan brown complexion and kept her hair in a bang. Every dude on the block, single, attached, and married it didn't matter, when Klareese stepped out on her porch, time stopped, every man froze, it was like a scene out of a sci-fi movie.

She would start walking down the steps; every man would start thinking about her in the privacy of his mind. Mine would be how could her jeans accommodate that entire ass. As she walked down the streets, any man who had a penis between his legs that was a real man, if only for a second thought about how it would feel to hit that.   That is talk on the real ladies. Even the married men, they probably would not hit it but they had at least thought about it.

I didn't know what she looked like in the house but when she journeyed outside that ass, hips and thighs, hmm hmm…let's just say by the time she touched the streets, she was a beast. A champion undisputed with the belt no skinny chick could ever take. I didn't know if it was the jeans she wore that exaggerated her ass or if it was just that big and wide. Trying to buck up on that could take a toll on a weak man.

Her mom would be on the porch giving every guy on the block the evil eye. I wanted so bad to say to her, "Excuse me Mama but that body that came out from between your legs got a whole bunch of dudes wanting to hit that. No disrespect intended but eventually somebody is going to hit that. Isn't nothing you can do except hoped he treats her right in the process." Of course, I never said it, always thought it in my mind's eye.

Klareese wasn't messing with anybody from around our way. It was somebody from out the way lucky enough to see that backside, wide spread and naked in a doggy style position. If I had magical powers I would have traded places with that guy,

YEAH RIGHT!

IF I had magic powers I would make her mine and hit it whenever, wherever and however. But since we live in the real world, the reality is I am just content to sit on the block with the rest of the guys, watching our champion rule the block.

Just My Imagination

Every day I see you come from a hard day of work while your man who has been home not making an effort to do anything sits back and I know he is getting all that loving. That good loving those big girls have tucked away up in between their thighs.

In my mind's eye, I have all types of ideas of how I want to hit that. I wouldn't love you like I had loved and made love to other women. Tailor made treatment for you, specially done just for you.

Those big legs of yours that command attention would get a lot of it. Daily massages with warm baby oil, a treat for the both of us, believe me! With that leg massage of course you would get complimentary kisses on those legs, all the way up to mid-thighs. No cartoon lines or lies would ever reach your ears from my mouth. The only bad things that would ever leave my mouth would be how I would love to sex you and make love to you and fuck you, all three different from the other.

In my mind's eye I see us slow dragging to a slow jam, my forearms on the sides of your wide hips and my hands gripping that fat backside. I imagine it squeezable and soft to my touch, in my mind's eye you tell me how your man can not handle it and ask me would I be up to the task. I tell you with you it is no such word in my vocabulary that means I can't handle it. There would be no such thing as too many times. I would hit five in the morning, three in the afternoon, early evening, and late night. I would make it happen and you would love the happenings I make.

I see you in my mind's eye asking me where we would make love. Let me make it clear, I could make love to you wherever you want me to: On the steps as you hold onto the banister, on top of the washer machine with it running on spin cycle, on the car hood, summertime in the pouring rain.

And if I were superman, I'd fly you up to the sky, lay you on a cloud, open up your thighs and eat you. My tongue would move faster than a speeding bullet on your clit, you would cum more powerful than a locomotive and your screams would leap over tall buildings in a single sound.

In my mind's eye, my imagination, these things would be possible but as the Temptations would say, "It is just my imagination running away from me."

Eating big plates of food and desserts

I want two big gallons of milk with my big plate of food.

Big women are a meal I could eat all day. Have my face all shiny and greasy with me licking my fingers because you are finger licking good. So let me put a napkin under my chin because it's about to get messy. I'm about to suck lovingly on a bone and eat naturally baked sweetbread.

I have no favorites because I love all flavors, satiny chocolate…French toast brown…yellow lemonade…dark coffee…mocha…white chocolate and the list goes on and on.

Big gals lay back, open your thighs and offer me your tasty treats.

Oh! I see you got on silk panties sealing in that flavor for me. Now let me pull that silk wrapper to the side and get at nature's first candy, the original sweet for the sweet tooth. Let me open up that thigh candy and lick all those hot spots, those right spots, that l dot, o dot, v dot, e dot, and watch my tongue connect them all and hit that g-spot.

Some want the soul food or the junk food; give me the big gal food. Give me the big gal milk, let me suck on your nipples like a pacifier and revert back to my baby stage…

Goo Goo Gaa Gaa.

I might put some crushed ice in my mouth, get the nipple of that breast chilled and then go down to eat cereal with that milk. Your fruity pebbles or in some cases your make me coo coo for cocoa puffs. Accept the generous offer to place my head between your thighs and see what's on the menu. And whatever it is, best believe I can manage.

Don't listen to these other guys with their empty talk of bullshit and lies. They are not hungry, they don't want to eat. They want to play with their food. Not me. I want to eat, I'm starving.

My tongue is the spoon and fork and sometimes a knife when I want to spread my tongue across the lips of your pussy. A spoon when I want to dip and taste the gravy from your pussy meat. Sopping it up without no biscuit, getting my face wet, forgive me I'm just a sloppy eater. I'm in nose deep, face down in it. So big gals, give me an invite, I am looking for a table to sit down to.

Hopefully it might be yours.

The Slow Seduction Part One

When I come in the room have it pitch dark. I want you in the bed naked with your legs spread wide open. Now rub your clit, let it get moist. I'm a smell your aroma like a blood hound and my nose is going to lead me right to your pussy. Have your feet cleaned because I am going to start by sucking your big toe, I am going to caress your other four toes using my thumb to lightly rub the bottom your foot.

Next, I am going to crawl on the bed...don't worry when I came in, I used the shower in the basement to shower and then I put my sweet body oils on. You smell them, smells nice don't it? I know, as I was saying I am on my knees crawling towards you like the Lion I am. I stop at your legs, I lick your left leg and then I move my head across and lick your right leg. I go back and forth, left leg to right leg repeating that action for about two or three minutes. It had been only light dry kisses now I bring my tongue in and let your skin experience some wetness. Now I lick all the way up to your right thigh, skip over your pussy, to your left thigh, and lick down to your ankle. I repeat in on your right thigh, every lick is slow and sensual. Now I kiss lightly up your body, get to your pussy and blow lightly on it but I am saving that so I move on up to your breast. I take my tongue and circle around your areola, your left one then I move to your right one and I alternate between that and flicking your nipple with my tongue.

Your breasts are large but I am taking good portions of them in my mouth, your nipples are almost touching the back of my throat. Next I scoop up some of the Rita's water ice, Cherry that I brought in the room with me and put it half melted but still icy and wet in my mouth. I push both of your breasts together and suck both nipples at the same time. I hear you're breathing becoming shallow and I feel your hands on my head. You bring my head up to your face and our lips meet, we deep tongues kiss as left-over Rita ice run downs your mouth. I catch it before it reaches your chin and then I bring my tongue around to suck on your earlobe.

I feel the sheets on the bed tense up so I know you are grabbing them. I hear you whisper in my ear, "You got me so hot Keno, I want to feel your dick in me, baby."

I say back to her, "I was going to do something special to you tonight to show you how much I care for you. I was going to eat you, get my tongue in between your slit and taste your pussy lubrication; do you want me to do that, baby?"

She, answered back, "Yes baby! I want you to eat this good pussy for me, please Keno, it is all yours baby. It has got your name all over it."

I go down between your thighs and lick your outer lips of your vagina, both sides before running my tongue in between and then up and down your slit.

I take my hard tongue and fuck your pussy as you grab my head and push my face in every time I pull out. I pull your hood up and start sucking on your clitoris; it's like sucking on a tiny Jolly Rancher. The aroma is exciting and the taste is making me lap it up like a dog licking out of his water bowl. I suck your clit and then long stroke my tongue up and down your slit, then back to sucking your clit again.

I feel your legs wrap around my neck, I help you by putting my hands under your ass cheeks and pull the pussy up so my face can go deeper and at least a half an inch of my nose is in your pussy. I rub nose and tongue up and down your slit, ending with me sucking on your clit. I keep that movement and rhythm going.

You're breathing increases and your pussy is throbbing against my mouth. I hear, "OH SHIT!"

And at the same time I feel your thighs tremble and your juices splashing against my face. Damn, I done make you squirt baby, you feeling me like that? I pull my face off your pussy and watch as you spasm on the bed.

I lick your juices from off my mouth and say, "Are you ready for part two, baby, my dick is feeling left out."

All in the Family Two

This is a conversation that followed the night after Fyah had tried to sex a sexy skinny woman and he couldn't get hard. I said to all that could hear the ears and all that could speak the mouth.

The eyes said, "Yo, that was some funny stuff, I seen it all. Tashi was limp, faking sleep and shit. I was embarrassed for us all as a team to see the look in that woman's face; it was eye to eye contact."

The mouth said, "What did her eyes tell you?" Eyes said, "They were like, damn! This is fucking unbelievable! This man walking and talking all that and he can't get hard."

Mouth said, "I heard all that stuff she was saying. I could not believe Tashi played us like that. As big as his head and ego is, I just knew he was going to stand up for the team."

Ears heard that and said, "Y'all know Tashi don't mess with no skinny gals. If she is not 160 lbs., no excuse me, if she's not at least 170 lbs., he won't stand up. He will fake that sleep shit."

Mouth said, "The hand should have slapped his little ass, *no offense hole in the back*, around. I bet he would have gotten all big and swelled up then. When he comes outside to pay the water bill, I am going to check him."

A half an hour later, Tashi came outside. Mouth said, "Yo Tash what's up with that stuff you pulled last night? You embarrassed the whole squad."

Tashi paid his water bill and looked up and said, "She said

his dick wouldn't get hard. Where's ears, eyes, and mouth in the word, Dick? Its all on me…my name was called not y'all. Eyes, you know what type of woman to look at and mouth you know what type of woman to talk to. So when you bring a woman home and I come out and if it is a woman I don't approve of, it's going to be the same thing all the time."

Mouth said, "I get tired of eating fish all the time, I would like a burger, but I don't eat meat and I don't complain."

Tashi shouted in, "Your ass eats pussy though don't you?"

Mouth said, "First of all, ass is in the back and yes there were a couple of sexy big women and yes I did eat the pussy but I did my part and we are not talking about me, it's about you."

Tashi said, "Well it's like this mouth and eyes, next time y'all come together and get a woman, dig it! Make sure wide hips, big back side and thick thighs…in other words, I want full-figured, big bone, heavy set, whatever you want to use, make it happen hear me? Now hands help me back in and to the rest of y'all, PEACE!"

Hand put Tashi back in and zipped him up. Mouth said, "He got a big ego."

Eyes said, "He got a big head too." It goes to show you, every team has a star player.

Keno Asking for a Number

"Excuse me Sister, no disrespect intended, but Rass! How can I say this, if you are single can you see some way to bless me with name and number? Name so I can dismiss sister and number so I can call you and get to know you? Now I don't want you to think I go around doing this to every sexy big woman I see. The fact of the matter is, I'm shy, a very quiet type of guy. I knew that if I let you walk past me without me saying anything to you, I would get home and regret it."

" Now they call me Keno but the name on my driver's license is…here, matter of fact, let me show you. Look it says Keith Waldo. My birth name but most people call me Keno. I'm single, rent a one bedroom apartment and work a forty hours week job out in the suburbs. I have no excess baggage, no crazy ex or girlfriend, no kids so I don't have baby mama melodrama with me. I do smoke ganja, I drink Heineken on occasions. I'm attentive, caring and faithful. I come with a no cheat, no bullshit guarantee."

" I am telling you this because I want to get to know you. Take you out and do things with you. *I want to put a crown on your head and make you my Queen. You can rule over this kingdom I call my heart and feelings. I love sports but I won't play games with you. I love to take in a good show but I won't take you for granted. Let me show you a new meaning to old things. Let me slam your bad doors shut and open up some good ones. Eliminate the bullshit in your life and show you there are still real black men out there.* Give me a chance to manifest everything I'm saying to you into a reality. Let me turn words into action because actions speak louder than words…as they say. Just give me your number and let me show you. Did Keno get the number???

The Response

"So you want my name huh? Why? What caught your eyes, my big tits, wide hips, or fat ass, which one was it? You better not say my personality either because you don't even know me. If you like big woman then it's usually something physically about us that you like. If you like big breasts then every big woman you see with big breast you are going to say something to. Same way with ass and hips. Is it because they say us big girls have a wet and gushy pussy and don't lie and say you never heard that because I've heard that myself."

"Look at you…you stuck trying to figure out what you are going to say next. You don't want to say anything that's going to mess up your chances of getting my cell number because if you don't get it then you can't get to know me. If you don't get to know me then you can't get to fuck me. Can't get to suck these fat perky nipples and squeeze these large titties. Can't get a chance to jump up in this wet pussy, even now look at you, you got an erection. You saying one thing but your dick is betraying your true intentions. I mean you sexy as…all get out…and you a dread oh, forgive me I see the red, gold, and green, you a Rasta huh? Your name is Keno huh? I love the name."

"I hear Rasta men buck up on some pussy and tear it up; all that roots man and Guinness y'all drink have the dick all strong and proper. Even with that said dread, I know you keeping a lot of women. Some of y'all Rasta men come like King Solomon and King David; they had a lot of women in their court. Oh, you different though huh? What makes you so…Damn...Ummm…your dick is just there…Damn! Alright let me get my composure because even if I mess with you, I'd be scared to give it to you. You look like you'll get ragamuffin on some pussy."

"Anyway, why should I give you my number, Keno! All you going to do is break my heart, sex me up all good and have me all fucked up about you plus Rasta and island men don't eat pussy or so they say. As juicy as your lips are it would be a shame for you not to eat pussy and that is one requirement I would ask if you were my man, not an everyday thing but sometimes in the week I want to see my man's face shiny with my pussy juices. I want to feel his tongue and mouth on more than just my mouth and tits."

"But since you came at me respectfully and hail me up as a Queen, I'm going to give you my name and number, here and put it to use sexy. Don't let my number be a stranger to your phone and ring on my cell."

She Need it Stronger, Harder, Longer

A woman called me last night crying, I had been in a deep sleep and when I answered the phone, I was still kind of groggy. I put the phone to my ear and asked who was it, and when I heard her crying it woke me up.

She said. "Keno, I need you to put your pants on jump on the bus, fuck it…catch a cab, I'll pay for it. The boy I mess with came over, got me hot and horny and then couldn't handle the job. I need you to patch up this fucked up work he done left behind."

I told her, "Babe…Chill! Men at one time or another mess up on the job!"

"NO!", She answered back. "He does this every time, it's either too fast, not hard or no stamina. I'm tired of this bull; this work needs to go out tonight."

Now here I was in bed, tired and wanting to get back into my sleep and rest. My penis on the other hand heard that and stiffened up.

I know what it was thinking, "Keno, that big sexy piece of woman needs us, get your ass up and let's go."

I thought for a minute, that weak ass dude done tried to do some work and couldn't finish the job now she wants me to come and finish something he shouldn't have started in the first place. He should have read my steps for dealing with a full-figured gal in the matters of the bedroom.

<u>Step One:</u> Small dicks and weak backs are a liability.

You better not bring those into the bedroom when you dealing with a BBW. You better come with a full clip of ammo ready to hit that. The bedroom becomes a playground and if you can't score the winning basket, keeps your balls and yourself on the bench.

"Damn Woman, it's raining outside; I am in bed all comfortable and what not. Plus he done been inside of you already, I don't want to come behind that."

She said, "No! That is what I'm saying, he was sucking on my tits and I'm stroking his small dick, trying to get it hard to put a condom on and he busted right in my hand. I got mad and put that ass out. So now I'm begging you to come handle this because I know with you I know I'll get that 'proper proper'."

"What could I say? She called Clark Kent and asked for Superman. There was nothing else to do but put on my super hero uniform and come to her rescue…up, up and away!"

Bootleg versus the Real Thing

He wasn't giving you love, he was just giving you dick and from what I heard it wasn't even good. Sorry ass dick and hard times is all he could offer you. You could have gone to the X-rated shop and got a dick minus the hard times. He didn't love your full curves, wide hips or heavy breast. His mouth never went down past your waist. Boy was crazy, how could he never go to have those big soft thighs locked around his head.

Me, even with your thighs locked around my head, I would have grabbed your thighs and squeezed them even tighter around my head as my tongue plunged deep to taste nature's first juice. I would have lapped it up like you see a cat lapping milk from his milk bowl but it isn't even about giving her oral pleasure it was about pleasing your woman. Showing you love her by your actions because actions speak louder than any bullshit words coming from his mouth. Yawl was fucking, not making love; that's the difference between having a real man and a fake man. You had a knock off man with a boot leg tag on him. Women get tricked all the time getting the bootleg thinking he's the real thing until they get him home and discover he either broke or he don't play right.

So I don't blame you but are you ready for the real thing. Are you ready for a lot of attention, caresses and kisses? Good loving, the kind that if you get it in the morning, you'll call off work but it's not the type of love that will tear you down, it will build you up. This is the type of love I offer to you. It has been on lay-away waiting for you to come pick it up. Now that you got me, try me on. I fit well on you; feel how warm my love is. I feel good with you and feel good on you. Nothing bootleg about this, I am 100% real black man.

Breast Sex 101 Part One

So many top heavy women that I know always ask me what's up with guys and titty fucking, I mean tit sex. I would be faking if I use the "F" word because I do not even use it. So tit sex, many bra busting women want to know what's up with it.

Ladies, that is the…I cannot even find the words for it, let just say, its that thing, that proper, proper, make my toes curl up. Now for me, I like the triple "D's" which is really an "F" cup or higher. "C" and "D" cups fly under my radar, now I hear you sexy big gals huffing and puffing your breath, hear me out.

85% of the women in this country don't even know their correct bra size. If you breast are bubbling out at the top of your bra or if when you take off your bra your tits drop almost down to your waist, well most likely you are past a "D" cup.

Now when I am with an extremely big titted woman, I bring a glass filled with ice and a little bit of soda. She is thinking I am drinking soda but I have other uses for it in my mind. Before we begin kissing, I drain the little bit of soda leaving the ice melted but still in big pieces. I start kissing. I am sucking her tongue and licking her top and bottom lips. I'm going from lips to neck to earlobe back to lips again, now I bring my finger into play and send them and my hand on a little mission right under her blouse.

With my right hand in the front under her blouse, I move my left hand under her blouse, in the back and unhook her bra. Now with my right hand, I push her bra up and those massive tits fall down. I still got tongue deep in her mouth but I have not missed a beat, with both my thumbs and index finger, I slowly roll her nipple and feel it grow in my touch. I don't even have to ask, she's already unbuttoning her blouse, taking it off and pulling her unsnapped bra off all in one motion. As her breasts dropped, I caught one and brought it to my mouth, even though it was bigger than my hand. I have a way in which I can handle two-handed tits with one hand. I use my left hand to hold her breast in my mouth and with my right hand, reach around and grab an ice cube out of the glass and ease it into my mouth.

Now I feel her nipple tense up as the ice hits it and my big body participant moans letting me know she is enjoying it. I soon realize why she is moaning, she has copied me, threw ice cube and tit in her mouth and now both of her nipples were getting ice cube tongue massage. She had coffee cup, saucer size areolas, that is the sexiest part of the breast to me, I love them when they are that large.

I whispered but loud, "Sexy, you got to let me titty sex you. I need to have your titties wrapped around my dick."

She said, "You like that huh?" I said, "Yea, that's my shot, I got to get that!"

She says back to me, "I want some dick in my pussy" I said, "I got you, you can trust me."

When actually I was hoping I could fulfill that promise after what I know is going to be a good nut buster. I let her breast go completely from my mouth and started undressing. We both undressed at the same time.

Now some guys use baby-oil but I found that baby oil dries up quicker on the skin so Vaseline is my preference and I put a nice amount on my hand and make my way over to the bed where she is giving her moist pussy of vicious finger fucking. I get on the bed and start massaging the Vaseline all over her massive breast.

I had never done it with Samantha before and I didn't know if I would be able to contain myself as I massaged her breast. I couldn't keep my eyes off of them; I needed both of my hands to rub and massage the Vaseline into her breast. My thumbs kept rubbing over her erect nipples. I tossed two of her pillows at her and said" put those under your head and neck." I needed her head to be elevated so my dick could go through her tit pussy and right into a warm and wet mouth. Now came the moment, I climbed on top of her stomach and braced myself up on my two arms and placed my dick between her two massive tits and she used her own two hands to trap my dick in.

Damn! It felt good, I loved this feeling.

I then started sliding in and out of her tit pussy. She brought her head up and opened her mouth and my dick had a double shot run through her tit pussy, right into warm her tight mouth. I arched up farther on my arms so I could stroke that mouth proper. Between looking at her large areolas and my dick going in and out her mouth and breasts, I couldn't take it. I felt it start from my toes and move up my legs into my waist and come out through my dick at full force. I was sweating so badly and my arms almost gave out on me, I maintained though and my sperm shot out like lava and gave her a pearly white necklace on her neck. It was at this moment I collapsed on top of her and stayed like that for about 5 minutes. I felt her pinch me and say "you got me?" I pushed up off her and when my eyes seen those massive tits again, my dick came right back to life. She washed the pearl necklace and got on the bed doggy style, it was now time for the back shot. But what I am trying to say is that full figured woman with massive breasts, we men love the tit sex period, just like all the other sex we have with you.

Sure I Was Born For You

I'm pretty sure I was born for the purpose of one day meeting you, of bringing balance into your life to be a good listener and good lover. I think I was supposed to be drawn to you, to hear the beat of your big legs hitting the sideways and catch the rhythm of your wide backside moving, jiggling, switching, whichever term you want to use.

I burn a spliff and sit back and think that I was supposed to talk to you and get in touch with your mind. Write to you and get in touch with your heart and feelings. Introduce my manhood and tongue into your sweet warm place and get in touch with your sexuality.

Pretty sure that even though I had never eaten pussy before, with you I was supposed to utilize my tongue in our lovemaking. It would make me able to connect with the wetness your thighs guard so dearly and tight.

Pretty sure you would turn me into a junkie for that love, the more you got on top and moved my dick to all your hot spots, the more I would become addicted to you. Sure that I was created to enjoy you and if I didn't have you, I would be miserable.

100% sure that when you stand naked in front of me, my Monkey Tail would get hard and stretch out like it was made of rubber band. Pretty sure that of the twenty four hours in a day, at least an hour of that is supposed to be spent inside your wet pussy.

Pretty sure you are going to be mine, your heart mine, and your sweet, sweet pussy mine. Mine all mine, a hundred percent sure, mine, mine, mine, and mine.

Do You Miss Me?

When you are lying in bed by yourself and if I know you, you got the lights off and candles providing a sensual and sexual setting. I know you think about me. I was your man, best friend, and lover and I attended all the areas in your life that needed attending too. And while you might not miss me financially or materialistically, sexually, and mentally, you miss the fuck out of me.

My tongue has wrote chapters in your pussy and my hand prints are still in your ass cheeks from where I pulled them off the bed and pushed my face deeper into your sweet pussy.

Kept it wet and slippery so my man wood could slide right in and push in deep.

I'd look up and you'd be moaning and biting your lip. I know you miss that! Your ears loved to hear the sweet things I told you, I know your new friend personally and he doesn't do that.

I know your breast miss me, miss my tongue and mouth because I got the best titty suck skill out there. I have trained on DDD's to M cups. Even now I know your nipples are erect and your areolas bumpy, they need my tongue to brush against them. Consciously, subconsciously, and even in your unconscious state of mind, you are missing me. My foot massages, leg caresses, back rubs, and light kisses included you miss these I know you do.

Your new friend might fuck you and make you cum but I make love to you and my tongue holds the clues to make you orgasm. My manhood fills you up, it moves around in you like the hand of a clock and when it hits between twelve and one, that's your G-Spot. Bingo! I know you miss that feeling.

Your new friend might make a connection with your freaky side but only my tongue can lead your thighs in the right direction, wrapped around my face. My tongue is the thing that can ring your clit bell and make your freaky side come out to play. Now I miss that myself!

Anyway, you know I'm the rain man , I turn your bush into a rain forest and the inside of your pussy into a waterfall with constant rainfall so that it runs all down your thighs and legs and make a dry place wet. I know you want it wet again, I know you miss that.

You want to give me

      the title back as your man

        but until you come to your senses,

           I know you'll miss

me.

About You From Me

Spread your legs and open your thighs, let your loving be my sink and I will wash my face in your juices. Inhale your aroma, and make my mind and manhood get hard. My heart will cum and ejaculates my feelings for you. They will squirt all over you and leave stains on your mind. You will want me.

You will say he fucked my mind and humped my heart and I will say, isn't that what a real man is supposed to do?

When I open your thighs and enter your open mouth and put my tongue in it, I want your heart to want me and your mind to think about me.

If you give me the "or" I will give you the "gasm".

If you say hold me, I will lay your head on my chest and caress your face, run my fingers across your lips and say only JAH alone can interrupt this moment.

You have only heard about or read about love until this point of your life.

I will show you the true meaning behind it; reveal it to you in its purest form…

unconditional and clean without lies and empty chit chat.

The way Adam and Eve had each other back when they were kicked out of the Garden of Eden.

That is the type of bond we would have…a physical, emotional, and mental type of love.

You will be my Aphrodisiac, your body would keep my attention but it is your love for me that would keep me faithful.

Your sexy mouth that would keep my tongue in it; your large breast that would keep my head on them.

Your thick thighs that would keep my light kisses on them and your womanly fruit that would keep my tongue in it.

You have something that will always keep me near you.

Believe That!

Trust That!

A Bad Habit

I got a bad habit when I am around you.

 I need to make love to you.

 I need to have my tongue in your mouth, my body naked against yours.

Chest to chest.

Pelvis to pelvis.

Penis in vagina.

It's not lust; it's just that I feel complete.

Like I found and joined with the other half and now I am whole.

I got a bad habit, very bad habit when I'm around you

I need to spread your fruit open and taste.

I don't feel right if my face is not wet with it.

I know something is wrong with me and that I need help.

But how can you rehab from sweet pussy addiction?

I'm addicted to you, shot the hell out of cannon.

 I tried and I don't have the strength to break away, your good pussy got me hypnotized or something.

Whenever you pull panties or thongs to the side or off.

It's like your pussy starts talking to me like "come here, get on your knees, open your mouth, now lick, suck, lick, suck, pull down your pants, put it in…push in deep…deeper….deeeeeeeper!

You have some sexual method of control over me turning me into a junkie And you are the only dealer with the drug.

I'm addicted to the pleasurable experiences I get when I love you.

Can't control my feelings.

My tongue and dick cannot be trusted when they are around you.

I have a hunger only you can feed an appetite only you can satisfy.

Something I thought I had control of.

I no longer do and it's all because of you.

This bad habit…

Very

Very

Bad habit……..

Remember That Time

Remember last summer me and you went on a picnic. You packed lunch in one of those old fashioned picnic baskets. We went to a part of the park that was isolated.

You felt nervous at first because you said on TV bad things always happened at the park. I told you it was because the victims on TV didn't have this and I pulled out my 45 automatic with a fifteen clip already in. You breathed a sigh of relief and laid our blanket down on the grass. You set the lunch basket in the middle and brought out lunch and a light bottle of wine.

I rolled a fat spliff, taking in JAH'S art work, His beautiful trees and breathtaking landscape. As we listened to the sounds of HIS water running in the creek. We both breathed in air different from the dirty and polluted city air we were used to breathing.

I look at you and then I look up in the sky and say out loud,

"THANK YOU JAH FOR BLESSING ME WITH WOMAN, AND FOR GIVING   MEN ON EARTH THE FEMALES KNOWN AS FULL FIGURED WOMEN."

You laugh and say I'm tripping. I tell you I'm speaking the truth. You say" I bet you say that to all the big girls." I tell you I have in the past but right now, I'm saying it to my woman YOU!

I tell you I'm hungry, you lay down on your back, pull up your dress and spread your legs and say "lunch is served." I lick my lips and say," I want to save that for dessert." You laugh and roll over your stomach, I like the way your red satin panties look on that fat backside of yours, DAMN! Your hips are wide. You reach around and smack your ass and say, "what about this, you saving this too?" I walk over to where you are at and get on my knees in between your spread out legs. I start to rub and caress your backside through your panties. You say "I thought you were hungry?" I tell you I'm still hungry, I've just changed my mind on what I want to eat. I continue to caress your nice big soft ass it's jiggling and moving like Jell-O.

My dick is becoming rock hard in my pants. You start rotating your hips, your pussy grinding on the blanket. I hear you moaning and I take my hands off your ass to slip my shirt off, unbuckle my belt and unzip my pants and lay my gun to the side.

While I'm doing that you are still grinding on the blanket. You tell me "put your hands back on my ass babe, it feels good." I do as you command and return to rubbing but with a little more pressure on your soft and big wobbly ass. I hear you whisper, "babe my pussy is moist now, it needs your tongue to get it wetter. I stand up, kick off my sneaks and pull off my pants. Your hips and ass are still rotating on the blanket. I look around to make sure no peeping toms are peeping at us, check where my gun is just in case and once I have concluded everything is cool; I get back in my knee position. I pull your panties off, my dick is standing upright waiting for his moment to shine but at the moment he has got to play back up to the tongue.

I pull the remainder of your dress off you and lay down a little bit above your head. I lay flat on my back and tell you to lift up and move up so that your pussy is right over my face which you do. Then you lower your pussy on my face with your arms outstretched and holding you firm. You start to grind your pussy on my lips. I grab your ass cheeks and move your ass in the circular motion like your hips are going. I flick my tongue up and down your slit and then I put my hard tongue in your pussy and with my hands on your ass cheeks, I guide your slit up and down, top to bottom on my tongue. I lick from bottom to top, pull your pussy off my lips and put it back down and lick from bottom to top again.

It's driving you wild, now I start sucking on your clitoris, squeezing your cheeks and licking on your clit with the brush of my tongue. You start moving faster, more wildly but my hands which by now are on your waist are holding your pussy firmly on my face and tongue. You start bucking hard on my face, my face and beard is wet from your juices. You say to me "babe I want to cum, I'm about to cum on your face babe…

OH DAMN...I want to cum!" I tell you not yet and lift you off and ease you back onto my dick. Your wet pussy slides down my hardness. I grab your ass cheeks and guide you up and down, your pussy lubricating my hardness and now riding up and down on it. You lean down and start licking my lips, tasting your own juices before putting your tongue in my mouth. I catch your tongue and start sucking it. Now you start grinding your pelvis into mine and I grab your ass cheeks and pull myself deeper into you. We're grinding in synchronized circular movements. We both are sweating and as I come close to ejaculating, I fill my breathing become shallow and quick. Now I hear you screaming out loud into GOD'S nature that you're Cumming and as you do I stop and hold you as you tremble and spasm, enjoying your orgasm. DAMN! I'm hard just thinking about it. Do you remember last summer in the park?

Going To Bed Alone

My dick thinks of you and is no longer under my control. It comes to life in my hand and hardens, it needs attention I grab the Vaseline and it slides on like its saliva from your mouth. My hand becomes a tight hole and slides down on my dick like your tight pussy. It rides up and down easily with help from the Vaseline. This is like your pussy lubrication. I close my eyes and imagine it is your mouth. I slide my closed fist on my fat mushroom head, And spend the next three minutes riding my head. Its feeling good, DAMN!

I need you but you are not here. So I settle for this good feeling my hand is giving me. Next I imagine my hand is your pussy and ride my fist the full length of my penis. I fuck my hand in a slow rhythm and notice pre-cum forming at the tip of my head. I pick up the pace and start fucking my hand fast and steady. Raising my ass off the bed to meet my hand. Now I'm slamming into my hand. I'm beating my dick and at the same time. Beating my hand up like one would beat a pussy. I feel pressure building up in my penis and pump my dick into my hand even faster.

My breathing is speeding up and then AHH!

Hot sperm shoots out and floods my hand.

I shake and shiver.

Not a great nut but a good one, but isn't nothing like the real thing.

This is what happens when I go to bed alone.

A Woman Said To Me

Keno I got something to give you, dread.

I want you to walk and roar likes a lion in my hairy jungle. And drink from my river Nile waters. I know lions don't bow but this is drink from my womanly roots. Now not many lions have lived in this jungle. And it is a privilege for a lion to be in it. To inhale the natural aroma that drifts throughout it. To pick from its tree and eat of its fruit. Will make you stand up. Your lion root erect tall like the MIGHTY MOUNTAIN KILLIMAJARO.

Jump and move about in my jungle. Watch my Nile waters pour out on my dry lands. And leave them wet and of course the moonlight, the night time. Makes the jungle come alive with noises and sounds of pleasure.

 Keno got something to give you babe.

This fat plump loving is stuffed in some sexy panties. Waiting for your hands to peel them off. Put that fat mushroom head right there in the middle.

Right on my panties.

Push in and rub your head against my panties. Let the fabric rub up on my pussy and get it moist. Now push it some more. Your fat mushroom head and the panty material is in my pussy. Now draw for your condom. Put it on. Pull my panties to the side. And slide that dick into my moist pussy. It has been waiting for you. Make me cum on your dick. So when you pull out your condom is soaked with my juices.

Keno I got something to give you.

Something to show you. Show why women will always have the upper hand in a relationship. I'm a show you these big legs first. And make your eyes get wide open. Then show you these fat thighs. And watch the inside of your pants as your small dick grows into a much bigger one. Yeah this something I got to give to you.

You gone want.

 You'll pledge your heart, mind and dick to it. Most guys' eyes are drawn to it. But I want to give it to you.

Bet you'll like it.

Matter of fact you'll love it.

Keno I got something to give you dread, something to give you baby and it's all for you.

I Aim To Please and Leave You Full of Moisture

Sexy full figured women make me run and grab for my pen. They inspire me to write the ways I would love to please them. The places on them where I would love to put my tongue. Tell them the crevices and cracks I wouldn't miss because I can't discriminate when it comes to a sexy full figured body, every part of their body deserve my tongue's attention. You easily influence my pen to write what my mind wants to do to you. Free up the sexually active side you and after reading me you'll grab for your man, dildo, fingers or just a cold shower.

I aim to please and leave you full of moisture. I love to see big backsides you can't climb over and hips so wide you can't go around them. That makes me manifest paper and touch pen to it and write words to make thighs shake and clits throb. Words like I strike my tongue in between your thighs on your slit and spark a fire to get you boiling hot and leave the inside of your panty material stained with evidence that I was there. As a writer I have an obligation as a lover of full figured women to bring out any hidden sexual frustration you might have built up and give you an outlet to release. I want your fingers, panties and pussy wet and it's only because I aim to please and leave you full of moisture. Let me give you the nourishment to satisfy your sexual hunger and imagine I am eating you and satisfying mine.

Follow the directions that my tongue would take on your body:

Your hands and body, arms and legs to your thighs and up to your inner pink carpet which I would love to shampoo with my tongue. Let my words be the key to large bushy or lightly shaved doorways. My pen will write and caress your ears and massage your eyes and make love to your mind like I would do to your body if I were there in person. My mind is a big gal lover's heaven manifested unto paper by my pen.

 A place where I talk about grinding on big women for breakfast, eating them for a snack, and making love to them for dinner. And like I said Keno aims to please and leave you full of moisture.

Love or Fuck?

I'm here interviewing love and fuck to see who is more popular among the ladies. To understand this interview, you must wherever you see the word me replace it with whoever is being interviewed.

The Interviewer: Okay who is more popular amongst the ladies?

Fuck: Women are tired of love they want to get me.

Love: You crazy you have 3 main positions, doggy, missionary and woman on top.

Fuck: You done lost your mind love, sometimes women just want you to rip off their clothes and get me. Grab their hair and me the hell out of them. That rough me, that ragamuffin me, the me game is the reason young boys taking these older women from the old head dudes and the old head dudes the one all in love.

Love: Yeah right women want me in their relationships; with me the bond becomes strong. Me makes a woman stand behind her man and be his backbone when he needs extra strength. When a man is caressing and massaging a woman that's showing me. When he's sucking her nipples and licking her breasts, he is me-ing her body, and when he is eating, licking and sucking her pussy, he's making me to them. In the long run Fuck can't fuck with that.

Fuck: Love the me game got women shot the me out. I'm the deep quick thrust, the smack that ass and make it shake, then make women run out and leave their men at home and come get their pussy me well.

Love: Without me a house is empty, it may have a cold body but not a warm presence. Me makes the woman commit to the man and the man commit to the woman. If one of them gets sick, without me there they will not be there for each other. A man can fuck a woman well and she might give him things, but usually after the fuck they won't have anything in common. But with me a woman will give you her heart, mind and all the good things between her legs.

Fuck: Me what you saying women want to get me.

Love: No women want me

Fuck: Me

Love: No me

Well there you have it ladies I guess this is something that will never get solved. Some women will chose love and some will just want to get fucked.

20 Sexual Reasons Why I Love Big Women

1: In a short skirt or pants, big legs look so much better than skinny legs do.

2: Big thighs excite me and feel soft when you caress them.

3: I love breast sex and the bigger the breasts, the better the sex and most big gals have large breasts.

4: Pussy gets extremely wet and juicy.

5: The areolas on big women are usually larger and that's the sexiest part of the breast to me.

6: When hitting it doggy style a fat wide ass just looks better, especially when you hit it and it jiggles.

7: Big thighs tight around your head when you eating a big gal are exciting.

8: I love the feel of a big body on top of me, riding hard on my dick.

9: I just love big women.

10: Why not

11-20 just repeat 1-10

Five Dots on Your Body

You have five dots on your body that I want to connect and make your bed shake like thunder and your bed sheets get soaked from your womanly rain.

First dot is your ears; my tongue would trace and lick the outside of your ear, lightly grabbing your earlobe with my teeth and then sucking it with a warm soft tongue. I would flick my tongue in your ear and then caress the top of your ear with my tongue.

When I feel your heartbeat speed up a little, I would move down to your mouth, the second dot. I would lick your top lip and then your bottom lip and then I would ease my tongue into your mouth and caress and grind my tongue on yours. Two or three minutes of tongue fucking and then I take your tongue in my mouth and suck your tongue. The way I do this gets women hot. When you grab my neck and pull my face and your tongue deeper into my mouth I know it is time for the third dot, your breasts.

This is the dot I have plaques and trophies on my wall for. If sucking and licking a breast was an occupation, I'd be wealthy. I take the nipple in my mouth without touching it. Now I suck your breast, same technique like I'm swallowing juice but I am not. Your breast feels good in my mouth and now I take my tongue and brush against your nipple. I let that build up and now that I am sucking on your nipple it is feeling good to you. Now I move over and do the same to the other breast. Now when I hear you sigh or see you lick your lips, I push both breasts together and put both nipples in my mouth and suck them both at the same time. This comes with or without crushed ice…With or without Rita's water ice. Depending on how long it takes you to say 'OH SHIT!' I move down to the number four dot, your legs and thighs.

I give your legs light sucks and dry kisses before moving to your thighs. I suck and lick the thighs at least five inches away from that place which by now is getting moist and giving off an aroma. That is telling me it's basting in its juices and almost done and ready for me to eat. But not yet I get back to massaging your thighs with my finger tips and caressing and licking them with my tongue. I look up and see you grab your sheets; I look down and see your toes curl up and then uncurl, curl up and uncurl. Now I know it's time for the number five spot.

The sweet pussy, the first fruit, and the good and wet, tight and moist pussy. I bring my face to your panties and rub my nose up and down in the middle. Your moistness wets my nose through your panties and I inhale the aroma. I hope it taste as good as it smells. I pull your panties to the side and lick your hairy, lightly shaved or bald side of your pussy. I pull your panties a little more to the side and lick from the bottom to the top of your slit, it is wet and it mixes with the juice from my tongue. I pull your panties all the way off. I pull your slit apart and give little light licks on your pussy like a cat when it licks itself. I lick light from bottom to top and top back down to bottom again. You are rotating your hips under my face and now you lift your ass cheeks off the bed and I catch them with the palms of my hand and bring your pussy closer to my face. I pull your hood back so I can suck your clitoris. I suck your pink pearl lightly and rub and push my nose in your pussy. I pull my tongue off your clit and tongue the bottom part of your pussy with my tongue and sex the top part with my nose. My big nose, rubbing up and in your pussy causes your legs to wrap around my neck. I stand up now, your body is off the bed and only your neck is the only thing still on it. I am eating your pussy in a wheel barrel style. I am eating your pussy and you are grinding it hard on my face, my tongue darting in and out your pussy. Now you grind even harder.

I hear you and feel your hips and thighs starting to tremble, they are shaking.

You're almost there, almost there:

 YES YOU'RE CUMMING

YES LET IT OUT AHH!

I FEEL IT RUNNING DOWN MY FACE AND SOAKING MY BEARD,

 YES BABE YES

RELAX SO I CAN PUSH MY MANWOOD IN YOU.

SPEAK

Speak to me with your mouth

Tell me what type of man you want me to be

 And watch me become him

 Watch me manifest into a real black man

 As original as Adam when JAH blew breath into his earthly body

 Become my eve and let me protect you from the serpents of this
world

Ask me what my true intentions are and I will tell you my needs
are simple

To lay my head on your big soft thighs and as we watch television

 I would rub and caress your big legs

 Speak to me with your eyes and I will see how you see me

You already know how I see you

 As a big beautiful woman who I can show love to and make good
love with

I would say use me as you wish but just don't fuck me over

Speak to me with your heart and tell me how you want to be
treated

 And watch me treat you as a king treats his queen, a lion his
lioness, Barak his Michelle

I would be conscious of your feelings and give you the attention
that would make your girlfriends go home and curse their men out
because they are not getting the same treatment.

Open your thighs and speak to me with your loving

Ask for my tongue, I will send it to you

Use it as you please

As a cloth to wash your body or as a towel to dry yourself off with

Take my head and guide my tongue anywhere on your body

Everywhere on your body

Except the back hole, that place can't get my tongue

But everywhere else of course yes!

Let my tongue bring you into first heaven and make you scream
out onto the streets of ghetto hell

Speak,

Yes talk to me,

Say you must be dreaming

And I will tell you,

These other dudes were nightmares,

It's time you had a nice dream

It's time you felt good,

Felt happy

Felt satisfied

That is one of my purposes for being on earth

Speak to me

Call to me,

The answer I will give to you will be a good one.

Cereal for Breakfast? Part 1

I came down the stairs one morning and (add your name) pulled up her nightgown and showed me her breasts and said "hey baby I got milk, what type of cereal you want to eat?" I looked on top of the fridge and then I looked in the cabinets and neither place had any cereal. I said "Hey babe ain't no cereal here to eat." You then pulled your nightgown off so that you were totally naked and put one leg up on the kitchen chair, started rubbing on your sugar walls and said "this cereal can be any type of cereal you want to eat."

ME: What you gone offer my first?

YOU: Well you can have my frosted flakes they're greaaaaaat!

ME: Hmm go on.

YOU: Are you coo coo for cocoa puffs?

ME: I might come back for that one.

You now still in the same position with your leg on the chair start rubbing in between your thighs.

YOU: I got these sweet tasty fruity pebbles.

I lick my lips; my tongue and penis are both erect

ME: Those fruity pebbles looking damn good, what else you got?

You start rubbing your pussy with a little more pressure.

YOU: Just close your eyes (sing the fruit loop song) follow your nose, it always knows, the flavor of fruit, wherever it goes to this bowl of fruit loops.

ME: Those fruit loops are looking good right about now.

YOU: Well why don't you come taste with your small spoon and if you like it enough, then you pull out your big spoon and use it.

ME: Yeah I like that idea.

 I walk over to where you are at and get down on my knees and put my finger in your bowl and start stirring my finger around in your bowl. With your leg still on the chair, you move your hips toward my finger and start grinding on it.

YOU: Damn! Babe this cereal is ready for you, you should put your spoon in it before it gets soggy.

ME: I love it when it's soggy; you know I make a mess when I eat anyway.

YOU: Well stick your small spoon in and taste your sugar smacks.

While you are still grinding on my finger, I move my finger in and out and start finger fucking you. You grab on the back of the chair and push your pussy deeper on my finger, grinding harder as I slam my finger in and out of you to meet the thrust of your hips.

YOU: Damn babe don't tease me, send me to work happy.

I let my tongue follow my finger into your pussy and start tongue fucking you and rubbing your clit with my thumb. You buck up against my face so hard, I have to grab both your ass cheeks and hold them firm in my hands.

YOU: OH! Baby please suck my clitoris, you know she misses you.

I start to suck your clitoris, I'm getting floor burn on my knees but I don't care. I'm in my zone, sucking that pink pearl your pussy shares with my mouth. Now your hands are on my head, you're riding your sweet pussy up and down my lips.

YOU: Babe I need your big spoon, this cereal is ready for you now.

ME: yeah that floor was killing my knees.

I get up and pull out Tashi and slide him right in.

YOU: Sweetheart you better put a condom on remember you said you didn't want us to try and have a child right now.

By that time I pushed him in and started grinding from the back. You take your leg off the chair so you can meet my force. With both of your hands still on the chair, I grab hold of both of your shoulders so I can grind Tashi into even deeper. I rotate my hips and grind fuck you.

 YOU: This dick feels good up in me babe, ride it. Yes ride Tashi deep in me.

I am holding onto your shoulders like I am riding a bike and feel Tashi moving all around in your pussy. I hear your juices smacking and popping as Tashi moves around in you.

YOU: Yes babe cum with me, yes I am Cumming, Oh babe Yes!

I feel my sperm shoot in you. I stay in that position, sweat dripping off my face. When I ease out of you, I wash up and make my way to work. Your scent still on my beard because that is a part of you I can take with me. So I always look for the morning because I know breakfast will be there waiting for me. Sometimes it will be on the table, sometimes not. Sometimes on the floor, sometimes on the couch. Breakfast is the most important meal of the day and I start mine off with cereal and I would ask that you don't mess with it. You drink yours from a bowl; I drink mine from a pair of big thighs. You use one spoon, I use two. I hope you like your breakfast because I love mine too. Good morning and good breakfast.

My Tongue Has Left the Building

You didn't love me; you were just using me for my tongue

You loved the way I ate your passion fruit

You came even harder when you saw my beard soaked in your juices

I am not innocent myself

I love to slide my hard tongue in and out your wet slit

Loved to suck on your pussy hairs and rub my nose on your clit

You might have dug me but those feelings left you once we were out of the bedroom

You only made your loving available to me so my tongue could be between your thighs

You didn't love me, I was just a face you could sit your pussy on and ride yourself to an orgasm

Said my tongue was made to order for your slit

Something about the way I could rub my nose on it and then suck your clit

We could never chill and watch a movie or play cards and whatnot

It was always can you get some head?

I was your baby when you wanted that

It was the only way I could be with you and see you anytime I wanted to throughout the week.

I just wanted a portion of you

Some us time, me and you time but all it ever was

All it ever became was head in between your thighs, tongue in your pussy time

My tongue's daily route traveled a road map right through thigh driveway

Parked right into your pussy garage leaving your body quivering

And trust me; I loved to see you pleased

Smile on your face

Body spasms and your juices running down your thighs

All over your backside

I loved to have your body arched up off the bed

Your ripe fruit pushed up to my face so my tongue could be deeper in your pussy

Not as hard as but more flexible than a dick

Your body just naturally pushed out your belly when I was around

Your body clock saying it was time for you to get ate

I am more than an A.P.E (accomplished pussy eater)

I am somebody who wants to spend my life with you

Have a child with you

Show you a loving family can be a reality

But all you want to show me is you love the way my tongue rides your slit

And my mouth sucks your pink pearl

Well I am going to put my tongue on lockdown

No more licky-licky for you

I am sure I can find some sexy full figured woman to love me for me

To love everything about me

And not just for my pussy eating talents

So until my tongue has left the building…..

Forbidden Fruit

I am going to let you guys in on a little secret.

If you are thinking of sexing her

Of hitting that

Look here!

My Tashi is a legend in between her thighs and in her passion fruit. I opened up her slit, took my tongue out and this is what I wrote in her pussy.

1. Every dick coming in here won't be able to get hard

2. Every dick coming in here will come to fast so she won't get pleased

3. Every dick coming in here will get 1 or 2 or both

That is the curse on her pussy by my tongue.

What was once passion fruit, ripe fruit has now become a forbidden fruit.   Any man who attempts to taste will taste sour.

I have written this pussy belongs to me; it is rooted by my tongue in my name. Let every dick that enters here experience discomfort and no pleasure.

No stamina and no erection.

It is decreed by my tongue.

So it has been written.

So it has been done.

As A Friend I AM Telling You

I have an obligation as your friend to tell you and bring shit out in the open. You know that sexy chunky piece of woman you have at home. The one you cheat on constantly, the one you disrespect all day every day. Well I am in love with her. In the deepest parts of my heart and farther back in my mind I am feeling her.

You don't want her so don't get mad because I want to give her good times, good feelings and good loving. You have been neglecting her; she has dry places that need to be wet again. The lawn has not been watered in a long time and I refuse to let you dry up that pretty black rose. She cannot grow in your garden so I'm going to take her and plant her in my soil. Water her with love and sweet words.

Bring her big sexy self into JAH'S sunlight, something you don't do, you would rather she stay locked up in the house. I refuse to let you kill her spirit and self-esteem. Men like you try to pull down the sexy full figured queens but at the same time pull yourself up and make yourself out to be some king. I refuse to let that happen here.

You are not sexing her anyway, but even if you were I know you. You're loving and sex game is done, sorry, and pathetic, I'm going to give her some good loving, trust me! You will just be a bad memory, a nightmare she was having for a lot of nights. A bad dream she was having in the daytime.

She is feeling me and has been since you started bringing me over. Loved the way my lips looked and imagined them all over her body. Well I aim to turn that imagination into something concrete. And as big and sexy as her legs and thighs are I am anxious to sample those and more myself.

Well I just thought as a real man I would tell you plus I promised her I would be the one to tell you. So now you can trick happy like you had been doing but she no longer has to put up with it. So I hope there is no hard feelings, but even if it is.

F--k it!

The Conversation Part 1

Dick came home to find his private space, his home away from home ransacked, ran though, a mess. He came back outside and saw the intruder. This is the conversation that followed.

DICK: I seen you been in my place Dil and once again you let me know you have been here.

DILDO: Look your woman came and got me, matter of fact she opened up her doors and pushed me no shoved me in and you know me, once I am in, I will run all up and down in your spot.

DICK: I can't really be mad at you; I thought once she had met me she could remain faithful and give me sole possession of the place. I thought I would be the only one with keys.

DILDO: I told you from the beginning when you first came here, the landlord did not like the place empty for too long. That's just the way she is, sometimes her 10 girlfriends will come though. 5 will open and hold the door open and the other 5 will go in and out, in and out until they make the property shake. But if they come and get me and all 15 of us, me and the 10 girlfriends get together, we make the whole property tremble. Damn near cause an earthquake.

DICK: So you saying you and her girlfriends will always come in when I am not here huh?

DILDO: Hey don't be mad you the only one get to enjoy it with her. You and the landlord both get happy and she really loves when you cum because you bring your whole squad with you. Y'all have access to the whole building, the top floors and the basement. Even when I am inside her she is thinking of you. Wanting me to be you, I am just a substitute for you.

DICK: But why do you leave it so wet?

DILDO: That is only because I will be in there and she'll hear you coming, then she will pull me out and when you come the door is already open for you. She will be so excited about you coming, she'll knock over a bucket of water (orgasm) so when you come in her floors and walls are all wet.

DICK: But you say she crazy about me huh?

DILDO: Dick you lucky some landlords make their tenants share their property with my cousins. They make you come in the front and send my cousins through the backdoor. Our landlord doesn't do that.

DICK: Yeah I couldn't play that, I never even use the backdoor myself; I'll keep my key to the front.

DILDO: Yeah our landlord has that backdoor for restricted reasons only.

DICK: Well nice talking to you, but I got to go back in, the landlord is calling for me.

DILDO: You know I will always keep your place tight and wet for you when you are not around.

I would say from this conversation that I can understand women might use a dildo from time to time. I would hope that they don't say I will stay with this and I don't need a dick. Remember you were put here ladies to give men companionship and for them to return it back to you. Do not get stuck on the fact that because the dildo gives you a whole bunch of orgasms, you don't need a man. I would hope you look to the dildo in the absence of a man or your man, understand though the dildo cannot give you love, attention, caring or a good tongue. Ladies! Don't give up the dick.

The 10 Pages

I wrote 10 pages of some hot erotic writings and let Deen read them. She couldn't get off page 1 without her fingering herself and it wound up being forever stained with her juices.

Deen left it on her coffee table; her girlfriend Pam read it and took it for herself. She took it home and stayed reading it and cumming on herself.

The pages kept her eyes on their words and her hands on her clit. She was wetting and going through at least two pairs of panties a day. She messed up and told her sister about it and her sister asked to borrow it for a day. But when she got it and read it, she knew she was going to be keeping it for herself.

Her sister was right; you couldn't read it without your panties getting moist. And when she introduced her dildo into the party, her hand, the pages and dildo behind her closed bedroom door became the norm. Her boyfriend thought she was cheating on him because every time he came home and jumped up in her loving, it was wet and his dick would slide in so easy. She got scared and gave it to her girlfriend Rachel.

Rachel said she wanted to see what all the fuss was about. She did the wrong thing and waited until it was night, took a shower, dried herself off and got in bed naked. She got comfortable, laid back on two pillows and started reading. By the third page when the writer was talking about eating pussy and writing the alphabet on a clit, Rachel had to give herself a good finger fucking. Before she finally went to sleep, she had read 5 pages but made herself cum 3 good times.

She woke up in the morning and before getting ready for work, she read page 6 and got herself off before jumping in the shower and then going to work. Rachel took it to work and left it on her desk. When she came back from lunch it was gone, somebody had stolen it. What could she do or say "Hey who took my 10 pages of good fucking and eating pussy." She had no idea of knowing that her white supervisor had took it off her desk thinking it was some late work Rachel was supposed to hand in. But once she got it back to her desk and read about tongues in pussy and a big fat black dick, well that did it. Her panties were wet and she locked her door, pulled her panties to the side and pushed 2 fingers in her pussy and stroked herself to a banging got to keep my mouth closed because this feels so good I want to scream orgasm.

Rachel's supervisor then took those pages home and started passing them around the suburban white housewives network. They loved it, a black fat dick, good sex and good pussy eating, PRICELESS! It was like a drug. White women in the suburban neighborhoods were being mentally fucked and sexually stimulated by the words of a black man in the ghetto somewhere. Eventually one of their husbands found out what was going on and ripped the pages up. But their husbands and other men were about to be in trouble because those 10 pages were about to be a book and hitting the streets and stores soon.

Miss Ass Out to Here

She use to walk and control the sidewalks with wide hips and oh did I forget to mention

ASS OUT TO HERE!

Jealous women use to roll their eyes and kiss their teeth and call her names brought on by hate. Old men would look and shake their heads "DAMN!" They would scream out when she walked by knowing they could not even handle that entire backside even if they had a chance to. If they were lucky enough to get in bed, in a doggy style position, she would probably break one of their old bones anyway. They couldn't handle if she threw all that back to them.

Threw what? ASS OUT TO HERE!

Young teenage boys use to freeze whenever she walked by. I know many must have beat themselves off in the emptiness of their rooms at night, just thinking about her. Hoping when they grew up they would be able to hit it, wishing she'd still have it.

Have what? ASS OUT TO HERE!

With dudes her own age she was effective in getting their attention when she wore shorts, cut off jeans, and short skirts. Her big legs would be glowing in the summer sun, no doubt aided by the Vaseline she had rubbed on them. She'd come by us and every man's penis would stand at attention. Every man around the way dreamed to have her on the bed in a doggy style position hitting that.

Hitting what? THAT ASS OUT TO HERE!

I got my chance one day. I found myself in a position I had only dreamed of. Laid in my bed at night fantasying about it. Luck would have it that on that day I had drank roots and burned a fat spiff. She was joking or so I thought and asked me to come in her gate. Said she noticed that I didn't lust after her like the others did, so she decided now that she was feeling horny, she wanted me to hit that.

Hit what? ASS OUT TO HERE!

Beginning of my End

When the police came they saw me sitting down a glass of Heineken in one hand and an unloaded gun in the other. I had unloaded it on the two lifeless bodies on the bed. Though the daze of everything that had happened and the Henny, I felt nothing, heard nothing. I didn't feel when they grabbed me and slammed me on the floor, handcuffed me and took me down to the roundhouse. By the time I came out the police car to go to the roundhouse, reporters were snapping pictures and putting microphones to my mouth.

"Why you do it?" they asked me. Couldn't they see the Henny had numbed me? I didn't give a fuck about their questions, matter of fact, I didn't a fuck about anything at this moment and my life was over. Actually it was over three hours ago when I came home early from work.

I put my key in the lock, turned and walked into the beginning of my end. It was a thunder storm and pouring down rain outside. That's why they probably didn't hear me come in but I heard them, heard my best friend's balls slapping up against my wife's ass cheeks as he fucked her in a doggy style position. I heard her calling out his name the way she had called out mine so many times before. I followed the sounds upstairs to our bedroom. I looked in and I knew at that moment out of three of us, two were going to be on the wrong side of the earth by next week.

He had his hands on her hips with his dick sliding in and out of her, right under a spot when I had laid my head many times after coming home tired from work. Then he grabbed her hair and really started beating the pussy up. DAMN! I never even grabbed her hair. I left what they were doing, went in the other room and got the nine I kept in the closet. Crept back downstairs with a fifteen clip already in the gun and poured myself a glass a Henny and drowned it. Crept back upstairs and stood back at the doorway. By this time she was riding his dick. I watched as she slid up and down on his dick. She was enjoying it, I know my wife. And him this dude was like a brother to me.

He knew the problems I was having in our relationship and he took advantage. I cocked the gun back and walked into the room. They both turned around and had a look of both…OH SHIT! …and we're sorry. It didn't matter, I licked every shot into their bodies and then sat right there laughing and taunting their lifeless bodies. An hour later I called the police and told them come get me on the day I will always remember…The beginning of my end.

Anything Coming out of my Mouth is Real

I'm not going to say some corny stuff like thicker than a snicker or the rest of those lines that probably should sound sexy but doesn't sound right coming from these dudes' mouths. I'm going to sit back and let them say all they need and want to say. That lustful vocabulary like, "Let me hit that fat ass baby…or that ass waiting for this dick"…or it so many I could go on and on. I'm going to let them pull up on you in their criss looking cars, jewelry shining like JAH's sun and say the same things they've been saying to every thick of full-figured women they've seen.

 Some guys you will fall for, some you won't. Some lines will sound good, others won't. You might believe them when they say they can give you the world, money, taking you out, dick and to some women that is their world. I say why settle for the world when there is a whole universe waiting.

 The universe consists of him loving you and not every other big ass, wide hip and large breast female he sees. Or he on a cold winter night with snow on the ground and the car won't start how he can take a room and make it into a sexy romantic island setting complete with lovers rock reggae and whine up on your mind as well as your body. The universe consist of him loving you and your kids as he does himself, of loving you and your family as he loves himself, of loving GOD and his mother first because only then can he give you true real love. Of you leaving the house in the morning to go to work and hearing, "I love you babe," and then coming home to a handwritten note on the table saying, "I missed you today and how happy I am to hear you coming through the door.

Foot massages and body rubs are in the universe. How can you love her body when its time to sex her but can't love it when it aches and is in pain and when it needs your hands to make it feel better with caresses and ball finger massages. If she is sick and a doctor is not needed, nurse her back to health. Look at her everyday like you looked at her the first day you met her. Plus with all these things and more comes the good loving, good dick, good tongue or in some cases just beat the pussy up or fuck me. Now what looks better to you? World or universe? So after all these guys have been screaming world in your ear, when everything gets nice and quiet, I will whisper in your ear and say come into my universe, you are wanted here.

10 Reasons for Eating Pussy

1. It's a meal you can eat that is not full of fat, calories or cholesterol.

2. Its not grilled, baked or fried.

3. You can never overindulge on it.

4. It is an easy quick meal.

5. It is open 24 hours.

6. It can be a meal, snack or dessert.

7. Panties, thongs and even boxers can seal the flavor in.

8. You do not have to put it on a plate.

9. It can be delivered or you can pick it up.

10. Different flavors and sizes.

Big and Beautiful

You make the word big a beautiful thing to say, as in big beautiful woman.

You make the word big a beautiful thing to look, at as in seeing a big sexy woman such as yourself.

You make big something a man wants to hold and have as his, as in having you.

Your big beautiful legs keep my eyes greedy and wanting to see more. My lap wanting to feel their weight and my hands wanting to rub and caress them. Pamper them with vanilla bean Vaseline. Your big beautiful thighs cause a ruckus between men on the avenue in the summertime.

You see men running into things because they are so busy looking at them and tongues drop to the ground like they do on the cartoons. There is something about a pair of big thighs plus something short as in jeans or skirts, that drives black men crazy. 75% of the time I think it has to do with them having their head in between them, that's real talk. Next big beautiful backsides and wide hips. To be behind a sight like that and see something like that, if your manhood does not salute something must be wrong with you. Just the thought of it gets me erect and fantasizing about hitting it from the back, my hands on those wide hips and moving slowly in and out you, DAMN! Make me want to bust just thinking about it. Proof is in the pudding, how many wide hips and big butt women do you know that are single? Not a whole lot trust me!

Big beautiful women with big breasts catch a lot of eyes and attention. I like enormous breasts, milk in abundance. Not handfuls for me I need more like an armful. If breasts were fruit I would need watermelons. I'm not for the artificial silicone puffed out breasts; give me the natural take off your bra tits hang down breasts. A natural phenomenon on the urban streets and if you ever get your head in between a pair and your mouth on them, it is worth the effort spent to get there. No A or B cup for me, give me tremendous breasts with large areolas and swollen nipples. I just love the diversity when it comes to big women. All I can say is keep making being big a beautiful thing and I will keep on looking.

I love you big beautiful women.